T0374081

Flash Dreams of a Career

By Charlie Alexander

Library of Congress Control Number: 2016911865

ISBN:	Softcover	978-1-5245-2700-6
	Hardcover	978-1-5245-2701-3
	EBook	978-1-5245-2699-3

Print information available on the last page.

Rev. date: 07/18/2016

To order additional copies of this book, contact:
Xlibris
1-888-795-4274
www.Xlibris.com
Orders@Xlibris.com

Flash Dreams of a Career

Written by Charlie Alexander

Art Work by Charlie Alexander

Flash had great hopes that his answer would come in a dream.

So he happily headed for bed!

Flash was dreaming of his choices.

"What shall I do…who should I become?" dreamed Flash.

Flash tried his hand at painting!

Leonardo Di Flashy

“Being a policeman would help protect people.”

And then Flash thought of firemen too!

“Firemen protect people and things too!”

“Don’t play with matches!” Flash advised.

Flash thought being a jazz pianist might be cool!!

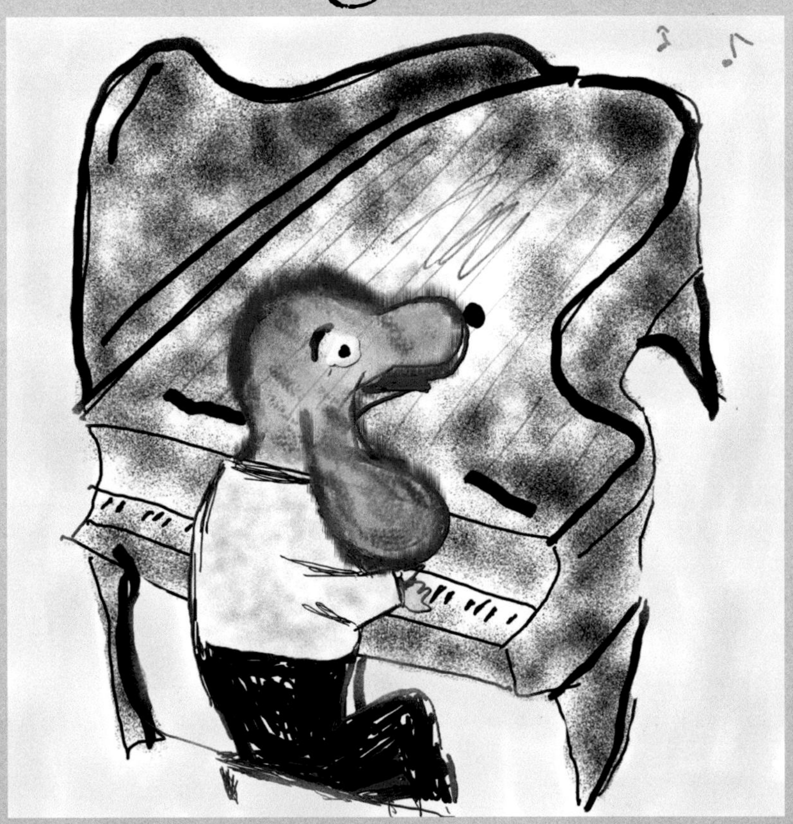

He knew Charlie is a jazz pianist!

“Becoming a professional skier might be exciting.” thought Flash.

He was in a hurry to pack his ski equipment!

"Maybe an ice skating star!" cheered Flash!

The ice is frozen solid.

"Or maybe a weatherman."
said Flash.

"Those people need some help!" reported Flash.

"I think flying a helicopter would be fun!"

The helicopter had just been filled with fuel.

“Maybe a professional golfer.”

Lots of practice!

"I could be a lifeguard at the pool." was the thought swimming around in Flash's head.

Great days in the sun!

"How about a job in construction?"

Flash thought about burying a bone!

“A farmer might be something to think about.”

The idea was planted.

"Or maybe becoming a doctor or nurse!"

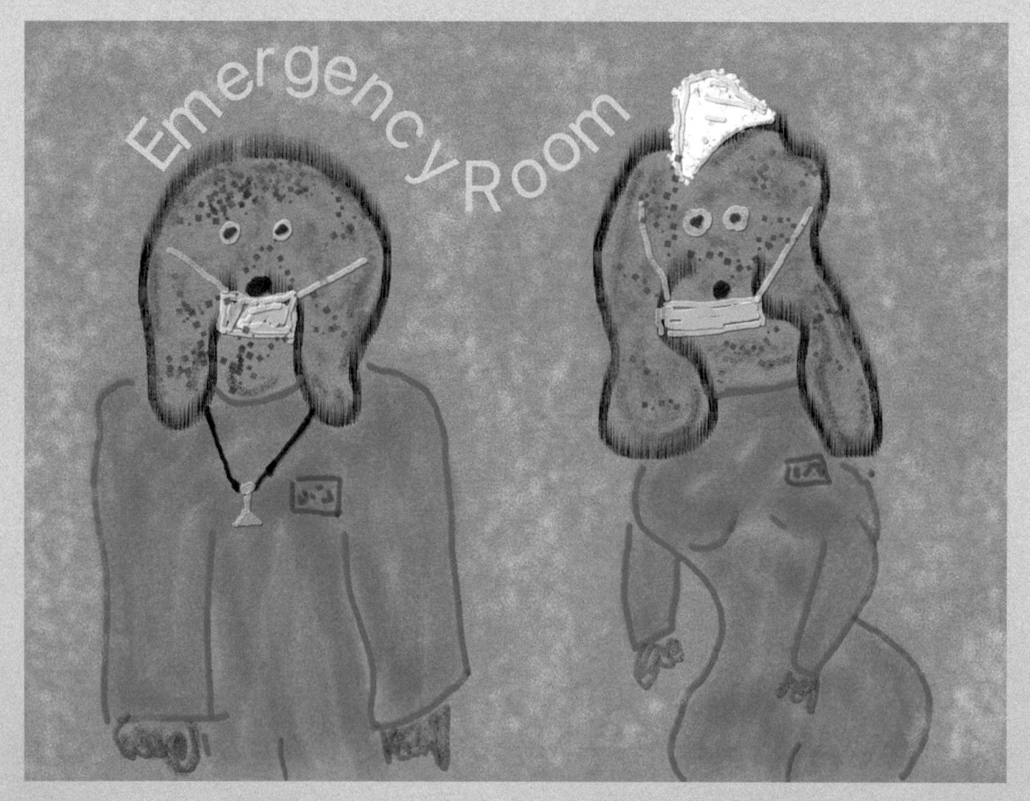

"A career in the medical field." Flash consulted.

"A military career is a possibility too!"

Flash would have to learn to salute.

"A card dealer at the casino would be fun!"

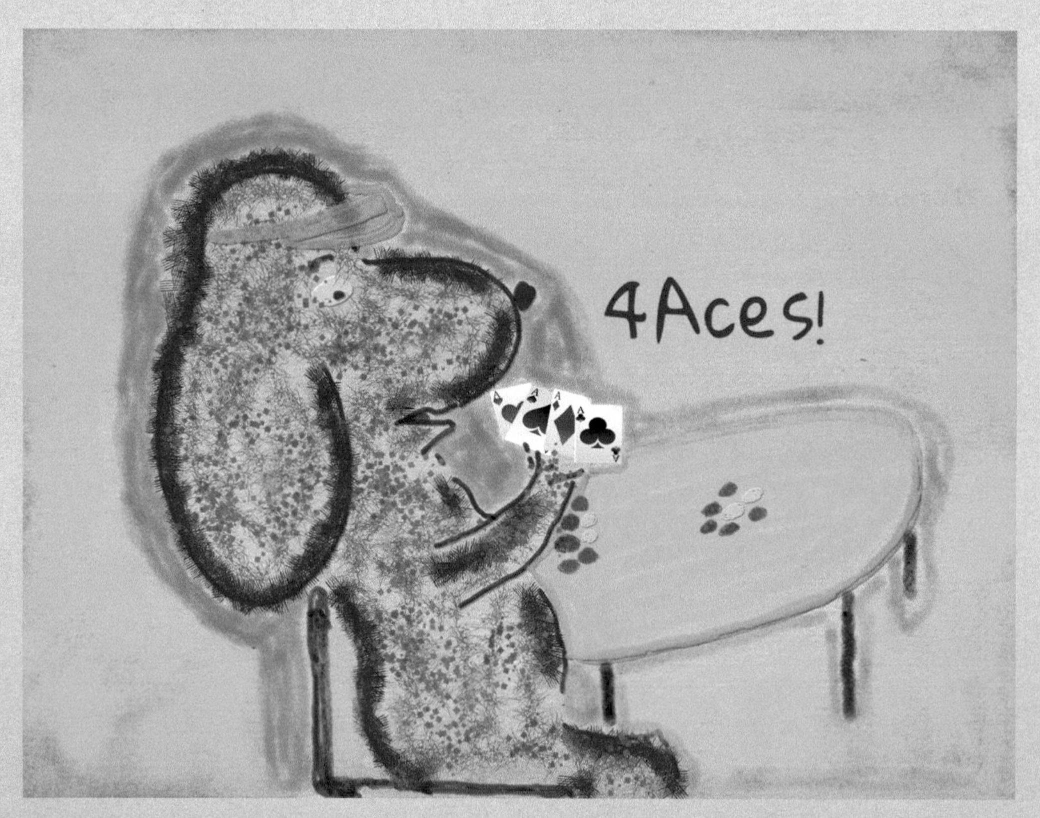

Flash's paws were pretty limber.

“How would you like to train elephants?” Flash was asked.

Flash had to pass because it only paid peanuts!

"I'd like to make ice cream and chill out!"

Flash likes ice cream a lot!

“If needed, I’d make a Good Easter Bunny.”

“It’s fun to give everyone candy!” said Flash.

“There’s a job building igloos in the want ads!”

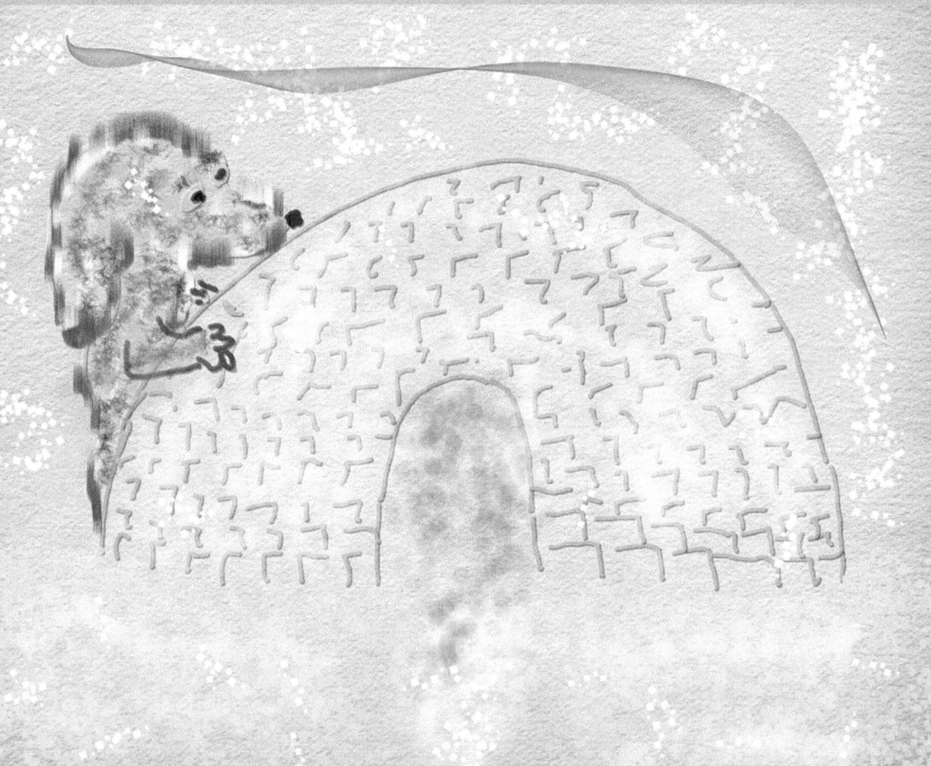

In Alaska-Real cold!

“Would I like conducting the orchestra?” Flash inquired.

“I can’t read music!” noted Flash.

Flash liked the idea of being a fisherman.

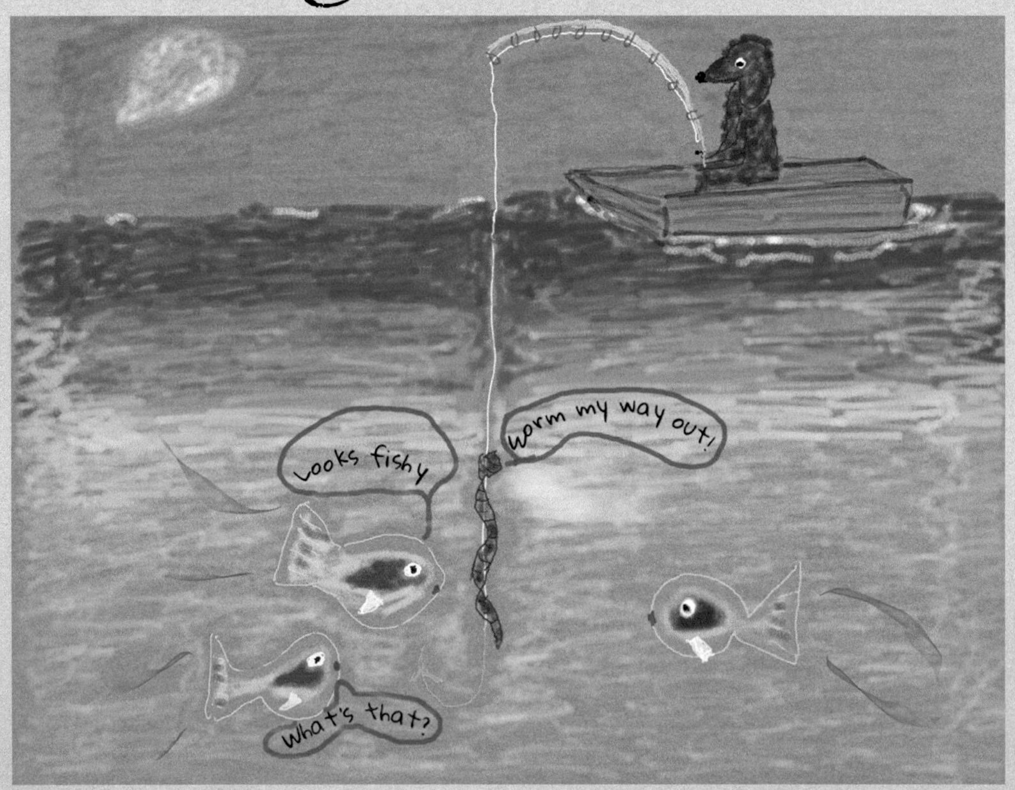

He wanted this job... hook, line and sinker.

“I do love fishing!”

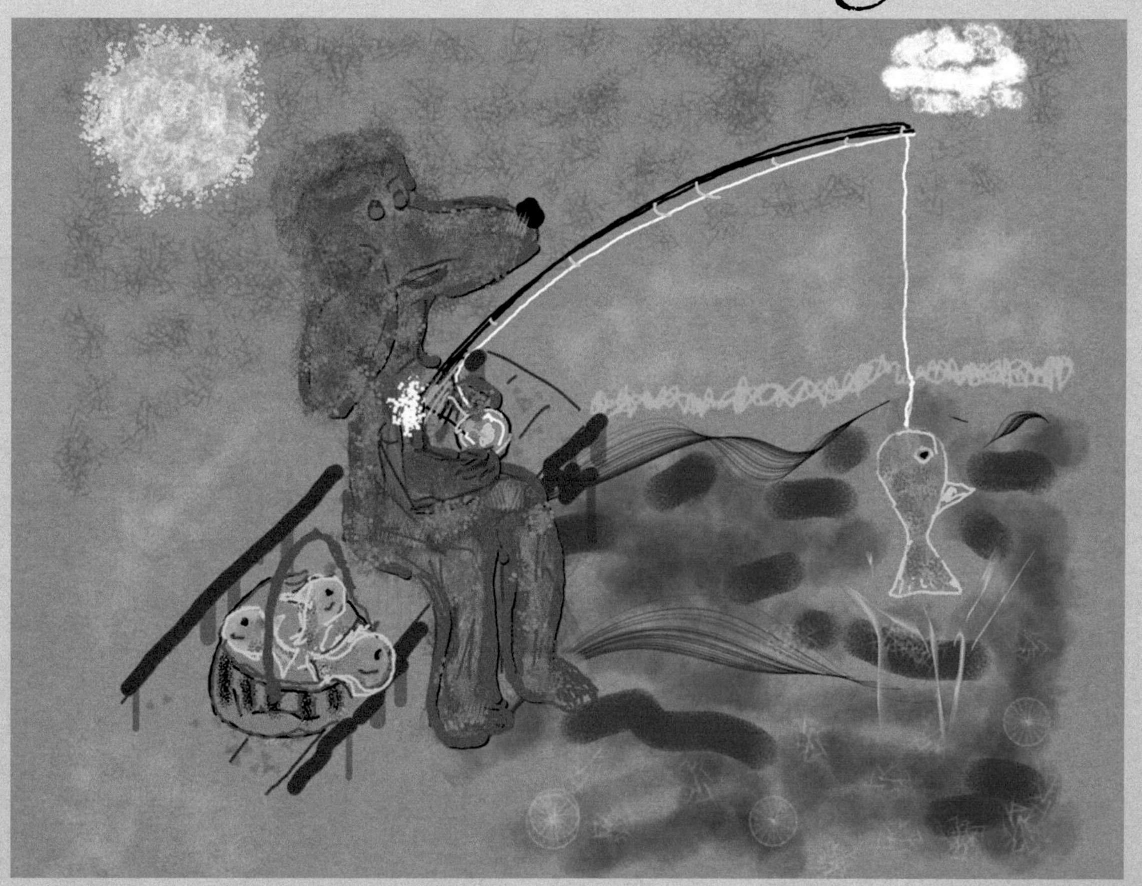

“Maybe not every day.”

Flash thought he could sell real estate like Becky.

It was harder than Flash had thought!

Flash was ready to join the Navy.

"Drop anchor on the port side!" ordered Flash.

"A photographer might be something cool."

"Smile and say "cheese"... please!"

“Here comes the judge!”

Flash really liked his cool judge's wig!

"I'll be a good dentist as long as I don't bite anyone!"

"The truth about your tooth..."

“Maybe a calling to
a religious ministry,”
prayed Flash.

“Peace be with you!”

“A bullfighter might be dangerous!”

“But I do like these pants!” claimed Flash.

"I could pilot a plane or even the shuttle."

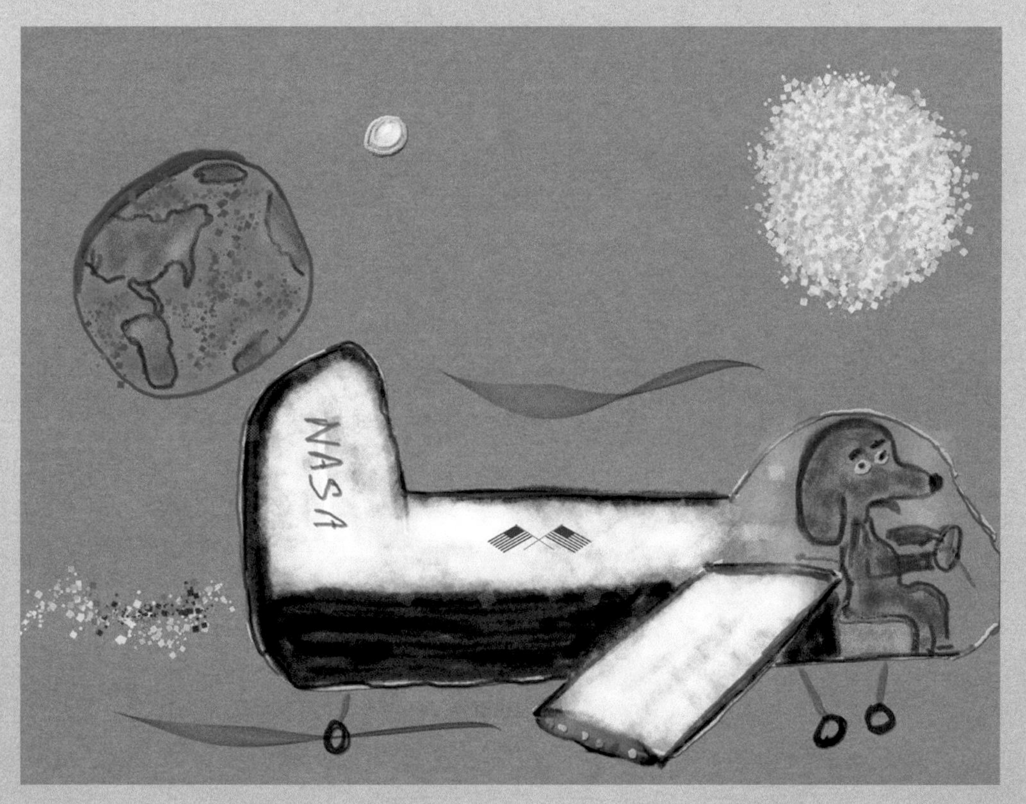

"I just need to learn how to land!"

A bank teller?

"It's like prison bars!"

"I just can't decide on anything yet!" said a bewildered Flash.

"I think I like being your dog best of all!"

The End

Printed in the United States
By Bookmasters